Chapter 1
Escape from the black of beyond!

Thomas Rickard lived with his Dad, Jeff, and his Gran, Whizz. Jeff worked from home writing Captain Crimson adventure stories for a newspaper. One summer it wasn't only the Captain who had adventures . . .

It all began one Thursday in the summer holidays. Thursday was Deadline Day, when Jeff delivered a new Captain Crimson story to the newspaper. Jeff usually delivered on time. But for the last few weeks, he had been delivering the stories late. So when Deadline Day came round again, Thomas went to check that Dad had the story ready.

Jeff was in his office, daydreaming.

"How's it going, Dad?" asked Thomas.

Jeff tried to pretend he was working. Thomas could see that Dad was stuck.

"I'll get you a cup of tea," said Thomas, heading for the kitchen.

Whizz was baking cakes. They were for the café where she worked. Thomas's best friend, Amy, was helping her. Amy looked up as Thomas came in.

"How's your Dad?" she asked, eating a fairy cake.

"Stuck," replied Thomas, pouring a cup of tea.

Thomas took the tea and a cake in to his Dad.

"What's happening this week?" he asked, looking at the drawings that his Dad had done. The last one

showed the Captain backed into a corner, surrounded by Krinklions. They were the Captain's worst enemies.

"This looks serious," said Thomas.

"It is," replied Jeff. "I can't think how the story should end."

Suddenly, the phone rang. Jeff refused to answer it. The answerphone clicked on. It was the Editor and he was very angry. His voice blared out into the room. He told Jeff to ring and tell him how the story was coming along. Then he hung up. Thomas turned to speak to his father, but he had disappeared. Thomas found him hiding under the desk, with the bin over his head.

Thomas went back to the kitchen. Jeff rushed in and told Whizz that he was going out. Thomas was horrified. He knew his father hadn't finished the story.

"What if the Editor rings back?" he asked.

Jeff told him not to worry. The phone started ringing as he ran out of the house. The answerphone clicked on again. Thomas's face fell when he heard the Editor's voice, shouting that he wouldn't allow another late delivery. He was sending a motorbike messenger to collect Jeff's work. If the story wasn't ready when the messenger arrived, Jeff would be fired.

Amy suggested that they finish the story for Jeff. Thomas knew how to draw Captain Crimson. He'd been doing it since he was little.

"But it's not just pictures," Thomas pointed out. "Dad hasn't finished the story yet."

Amy wasn't going to let that stop them.

"We'll imagine what he'd do to get out of trouble."

3

Whizz said they had nothing to lose.

"Except Dad's job," added Thomas.

"But he's in danger of losing that anyway," Whizz reminded him.

"Hurry!" Amy told them. "There isn't much time!"

And where was Jeff while the others were trying to help him? He was in the library, gazing at Gina Clough, the librarian. That's why Jeff couldn't do any work. That's why he kept disappearing from the house for hours at a time. He was going to the library to stare at Gina. He was in love with her and it was agony, because Jeff was too shy to talk to her.

While Jeff worried about how to make Gina notice him, Thomas, Amy and Whizz were working really hard to finish the story. At last, they were on the final picture. Suddenly, there was a screech of brakes outside. Amy rushed to the window.

"The bike's here!" she cried.

"It can't be!" wailed Thomas. "The Captain hasn't escaped from the Krinklions yet."

Thomas spun round to look out the window. His elbow knocked over a bottle of ink. The top flew off and a shiny black pool of ink spread all over the last empty picture box.

"Oh no!" Thomas howled. "What are we going to do now?"

Amy gave a strangled cry. "And your Dad's back!"

Thomas felt sick as he looked at the inky puddle in front of him. Then he started laughing.

"I've got it!" he said, pointing at the black picture box. "It's a black hole."

Amy thought Thomas had gone bonkers.

"That's how Captain Crimson escapes," Thomas explained. "Through a black hole in space!"

Now Amy thought Thomas was a genius.

Jeff flew into the room, running round in a panic because he hadn't finished the story. Thomas told Dad that he, Amy and Whizz had finished the story for him. Jeff stopped flapping. He was very grateful and couldn't wait to hear it.

When Thomas had finished telling the story, Jeff started dancing round his office. He adored the clever ending. The messenger took the story away. The Editor was very pleased with the work. Jeff's job was safe. Everyone was happy.

Captain Crimson and the crew of the starship *The Galileo* were patrolling through space, when First Officer Optic picked up a distress signal.

Captain! There's a Mayday call from Zenthurion Three.

Chief Engineer Widget slammed *The Galileo's* thrusters into High Space Overdrive.

ZENTHURION THREE

Little did Captain Crimson realise that he was heading straight into a deadly trap.

Commander Krinklion was Captain Crimson's arch-enemy. She intended to crinkle Captain Crimson into a trillion, lifeless pieces.

The *Galieo* is approaching, Your Krinkliness.

Captain Crimson was suspicious. The Mayday signal had disappeared. He took a landing party and beamed down to the planet's surface.

Suddenly, a cluster of Krinklions sprang out at them.

There's no escape, Crimson – prepare to perish!

Why should I? I want to see your utter destruction.

Take me, but let my ship and crew go free!

WHIRR

This will pour cold water on your plans. Go all of you. Go!

SPLOOSH!

Now for a quick escape!

A black hole had suddenly appeared.

Nobody had ever risked going into a black hole before, but it was the Captain's only hope.

GLOOP!

So, our space hero outwitted the Krinklions and lived to fight another day.

Curses! Foiled again!

Later that day, Thomas went back into Dad's office. He wanted to make sure that all the spilt ink had been mopped up. Suddenly, he heard a strange, gloopy, sucking sort of noise. He looked across the room and couldn't believe his eyes. In the corner was a life-size cardboard cut-out of Captain Crimson. It had been there for ages. That was where the noise was coming from. The cut-out was surrounded by a cloud of mist. Tiny dots of light sparkled all over it. Then the cardboard figure went all fuzzy and fizzy round the edges . . . and out strolled Captain Crimson! Thomas's mouth fell open. His eyes were as big as saucers.

"Health and happiness," the Captain greeted Thomas politely. "What planet is this?"

Chapter 2
Guzzle trouble

Thomas was amazed that Captain Crimson had come to life. The only person he told about it was Amy. The Captain said he'd be gone before anyone else found out. He kept trying to contact his spaceship, *The Galileo*, but he couldn't get through. The Captain liked it at Thomas's house. They had real food there, which was miles better than the food pills they ate on *The Galileo*. Once Captain Crimson discovered food, he didn't want to stop eating.

One morning, Thomas had just made Captain Crimson some toast, when they heard Jeff coming downstairs.

"Hide!" hissed Thomas. Captain Crimson ducked under the table and was hidden by a long tablecloth.

"Hi, Dad," said Thomas, innocently, as Jeff came into the room.

Jeff opened the fridge. "What on earth is that doing there?" he asked, reaching for something hidden behind the orange juice. It was a cookery book. Somebody had taken a big bite out of it.

"Oh no," Jeff groaned.

Thomas realised what must have happened. Captain Crimson had seen the picture of food on the front cover and tried to eat it.

"Oh dear," Thomas said.

Jeff was very upset. He'd borrowed the book from the library. He told Thomas that his life was ruined.

"She'll think I did it," he gasped, collapsing into a chair.

Thomas demanded to know who 'she' was. That's when he found out that Dad had fallen in love with Gina Clough, the librarian. Now he understood why Dad couldn't do any work.

Jeff decided to take the book back to the library.

"But it's Deadline Day," Thomas reminded him. "You have to finish your Captain Crimson story."

"You can't finish something you haven't started," Jeff replied, heading for the front door.

Captain Crimson poked his head out from under the tablecloth.

"Would this be a good time to get something to eat?" he asked.

Amy came round and Thomas told her that Jeff had gone out without finishing his work. The Captain jumped to his feet.

"I shall write this week's story," he told them. "Who better to write a Captain Crimson story than the hero himself?"

They couldn't argue with that, so the three of them tried to decide what to write about. The Captain said the story should be about a food shortage on board *The Galileo*.

At the library, Jeff was showing the damaged book to Gina. She was furious. She glared at the big bite mark. Then she glared at Jeff, because she thought he'd done it. He promised her that he'd found it like that and begged her to accept his apology. He gave her £20 to buy a new copy of the book. Gina said she was sorry for losing her temper and hoped she hadn't put him off coming to the library. Jeff's legs felt like jelly as he left the library. Gina Clough had finally noticed him!

Thomas, Amy and the Captain had made up a story about a man-eating Mogolith. They'd just reached the end, when they heard Jeff arrive home. As he came into the room, the Captain ducked behind an armchair. Jeff was worried about getting the Captain Crimson story finished.

"We didn't want you to get into trouble," said Thomas nervously, "so we had a go."

Jeff was delighted.

"This looks brilliant!" he told them, as he read their story.

Disaster had struck *The Galileo*. A fire had raged through the food storage compartment and left the crew without food.

here's nothing left feed the crew!

The nearest food-bearing planet was Plattos Nine, but it was three cosmic light years away.

At last *The Galileo* reached Plattos Nine. First Officer Optic showed everyone which food was safe to eat.

What's happening, Captain?

Suddenly, the landing party heard a distant rumbling. The ground shook and the trees quivered.

Hold tight – it could be an earthquake!

Beware! It's a man-eating Mogolith! Nobody move!

The Mogolith lowered his huge head and rubbed his tusk against the tree trunk.

Help me, Captain! I'm falling!

I'll save you, Dr Laser.

Captain Crimson quickly unwound his Superstrength Boomerang Rope.

I'll deal with this, while you pull Dr Laser clear.

The Captain was tugging at something inside the Mogolith's mouth.

There, there, Big Fella. We'll soon have you sorted.

The Captain pulled out a rotten tooth and the Mogolith stopped roaring immediately.

If in doubt, whip it out.

The Mogolith was so grateful to have his toothache cured. He helped Captain Crimson and the landing party gather enough food to last them on their journey back to Starbase.

No need for thanks, my whiskery friend. It's all in a day's work!

Jeff was very pleased with the story. He gave Thomas and Amy some money so they could have tea at the café where Whizz worked. Captain Crimson wanted to go, but Thomas told him that it was far too risky. The Captain refused to be left out of any outing that involved food. He followed Thomas and Amy to the café. He waited until they'd sat down, then slipped inside.

The waitress showed Captain Crimson to a table. She gave him a menu. There was such a big choice that he couldn't decide what to have, so he decided to order all of it. The waitress could hardly get all the food onto the table. Captain Crimson thought it looked wonderful. He tried to stuff as much of it into his mouth as possible. It wasn't a pretty sight.

"Sounds like somebody's enjoying their food,"
Thomas said to Amy. Then they stared at each other
in horror.

"Oh no!" they both said at once, looking round.
There was Captain Crimson sitting behind them, looking
rather poorly.

The waitress arrived with the bill. Captain Crimson
didn't realise that you had to pay for what you'd eaten.
He had never paid in Thomas's house. And he didn't
have any money. Thomas and Amy were trying to
decide what to do, when Whizz appeared.

"Do you know this man?" she asked sternly.

"Of course they know me," answered the Captain,
getting to his feet. "I am Captain Crimson."

The Captain bowed and kissed Whizz's hand. Whizz
gave Thomas a very fierce look. He knew he was in deep
trouble.

"Whizz," cried Thomas, "I can explain everything!"

Chapter 3
Banana drama

Once Whizz understood about the Captain, she was fine about it. And she agreed with Thomas that they shouldn't tell Jeff. Thomas felt much better now that Whizz knew his secret. And it was easier having someone to help keep Captain Crimson hidden.

Then Deadline Day rolled round again. Thomas went to see how Dad was getting on. He should have been working, but he was drawing pictures of Gina instead. Jeff suddenly leapt up out of his chair.

"Gina works in a library!" he shouted, skipping round the room. "So she must love words. Poems are full of words." He stopped prancing about. "I shall write Gina a poem," he declared grandly.

Thomas asked Jeff when he was going to write the Captain Crimson story. Jeff promised to do it as soon as he'd written the poem. Thomas said that he and Amy would go to work with Whizz, so Jeff could write his poem in peace.

Thomas and Amy were on their way to the café with Whizz and Captain Crimson, when Whizz remembered that she had to go to the bank. There was a long queue at the bank. They had to wait ages before they reached the front of it. Then, a big beefy-looking man pushed in front.

"Excuse me, Sir," said the Captain politely, "but the queue starts at the other end."

"Oh yeah?" the man snarled, rudely. "Well, the robbery starts here!"

All the customers gasped and stood well back. The robber put a bag on the counter and ordered the cashier to fill it with money. Police sirens wailed in the distance

as the robber forced the Captain to leave the bank with him. A battered motorbike was parked outside.

"Quick!" the robber said. "You drive."

The Captain sat on the bike. The robber climbed on behind him. Captain Crimson had never driven a motorbike before. He turned on the ignition.

"Thrusters into High Space Overdrive and away!" he yelled. The engine roared into life and the Captain shot off down the road.

The police arrived at the bank. They promised they would find the Captain.

"Don't worry about your friend," the Inspector told Thomas, Whizz and Amy. "The squad cars are in hot pursuit."

Captain Crimson and the robber sped along on the motorbike. The sirens grew louder and louder as more and more police cars joined the chase. Captain Crimson told the robber to give himself up.

"Never!" he shouted.

The Captain noticed a huge bridge that stretched over a large, deep river. The bridge started to open in the middle as the Captain drove onto it. The robber was terrified.

"Look out, Captain!" he shrieked. "There's water down there!"

"Really?" said Captain Crimson, coolly. "I'm not sure I shall be able to stop in time."

The robber gave a loud sob, then confessed that he couldn't swim. Shaking with fright, he agreed to give himself up.

The Captain put on the brakes. In fact, he braked so hard that the robber flew off the back of the bike. He sailed over the Captain's head and landed in the arms of a line of waiting policemen. The Police Chief thanked the Captain.

"No need for thanks, Chief," insisted Captain Crimson, modestly. "It's all in a day's work."

Meanwhile, Jeff sat in the library, trying to write his poem. He wasn't getting on very well. There was a tramp asleep in the chair next to him. Suddenly, the tramp woke up and helped Jeff to finish his poem. Gina told them off for making too much noise. She asked them to leave. The tramp begged Gina to let Jeff stay. Gina looked at Jeff's sad face.

"Oh, very well," she said.

The tramp nudged Jeff. Jeff stood up and nervously recited his poem to Gina. At the end, everyone in the library started clapping. Jeff felt very pleased with himself.

"Thank you very much," said Gina in a brisk voice. "Now, I really must ask you to leave." Gina held the library door open as Jeff walked miserably away.

"Thanks again for the poem," she called after him. "It was very sweet of you."

Jeff could hardly believe his ears – Gina wasn't cross with him, after all!

After all the excitement of the robbery, Whizz, Thomas, Amy and the Captain went home. Jeff was nowhere to be found. Thomas knew they would have to write a story for his father. Whizz agreed. They were all still thinking about the robbery, so they decided to write a story about Captain Crimson outwitting a gang of pirates. The Captain started boasting.

"Pirates?" he scoffed. "I could defeat them with both hands tied behind my back and my pants on fire!"

The *Galileo* was transporting a precious cargo bound for Stevenson Two. The treasure was too valuable for anyone other than Captain Crimson to deliver.

Maintain two minutes radio silence, Optic.

Entering the planet's orbit, Sir.

I don't like it, Captain. It's too quiet out there.

The crew were uneasy as they beamed down the treasure.

Suddenly, a desperate band of reckless space pirates came hurtling towards them.

Not on your life!

Hand over the treasure!

SPLAT!

Before the crew could recover, the space pirates had escaped with their ill-gotten gains.

You won't get away with this! Captain Crimson will stop you.

He'll never catch us!

The pirates were furious that Captain Crimson had ruined their plan. They lunged at the Captain and a desperate duel ensued.

But the motley crew were no match for the swashbuckling Captain!

Now that Captain Crimson had captured Long John Laserlegs and his unsavoury crew, he could safely deliver the real cargo.

Chapter 4
A giant celebration

It was Amy's birthday and Thomas had to tell the Captain that he couldn't go to the party. It would be impossible to hide a Space Crusader at a party for ten-year-olds. The Captain felt very left out. He sulked in Thomas's bedroom, while Thomas helped Whizz make the food for the party.

Jeff burst into the kitchen and started eating the sausages that Whizz had just cooked.

"Haven't you got some work to do?" asked Whizz. She smacked Jeff's hand away from the food.

"I've done it," he told her, proudly.

Thomas couldn't believe his ears! Dad had actually finished this week's Captain Crimson story. Whizz sent Jeff to fetch Amy's birthday cake from the café.

Suddenly, there was a roar from Jeff's office. Thomas opened the door and found Captain Crimson pacing up and down.

"Have you seen this?" the Captain stormed, pointing at Jeff's desk.

"Not yet," replied Thomas.

"Your father's drawn smiling flowers and little fluffy bunnies," he bellowed.

Thomas explained that Dad was very happy, so he'd

made the story happy, too. Captain Crimson didn't want to be the hero of a happy story. He wanted it to be an exciting one. When Thomas read what Dad had written, he had to agree that it was a bit soppy. So the two of them started work on a new story. Captain Crimson decided that he wanted to fight a giant. Thomas thought that was a splendid idea.

The *Galileo's* water tank had sprung a leak and they were desperate to refill it. So they made an emergency landing on an unexplored planet.

The crew were surrounded by brown, slimy grass and mouldy leaves that had been sweating in the heat.

What a hideous planet!

Let's get the water and go.

CLOMP! CLOMP! CLOMP!

SHUDDER!

What on earth is that?

It's a giant!

Suddenly, there was a noise like thunder and the ground began to shake.

The landing party gasped as a megamonstrous boot appeared.

The Captain explained the urgency of their mission.

The giant's massive hand swooped down and snatched the landing party from the ground.

If you want water, you must fight me for it!

Gotcha! Now what are you doing here?

As the noble Captain prepared to fight, his capable crew escaped to put his plan into action.

One stumble and you're mine!

The nimble Captain was too quick for the lumbering giant.

Down here, Big Fella!

As the landing pods flew in low, the Captain put his part of the plan into action.

Ooch! Ow! Eurgh!

With expert skill, the crew hooked onto the giant's strawberry net.

Steady as she goes, men!

Thanks for saving us!

No need for thanks, Optic. It's all in a day's work!

Jeff was waiting in the café for the waitress to fetch Amy's cake. Then he saw Gina outside. Horror of all horrors – she was with another man! Jeff hid as Gina and the man came into the café and sat down. He was broken-hearted.

"Gina – with another man?" whimpered Jeff. "My life is over."

By the time Thomas and the Captain had finished the story, Whizz was ready to leave for the party. As she was packing the car with food, Jeff arrived home. He was very sad, but he wouldn't say what was wrong. Whizz was cross that Jeff had come home without Amy's cake. She made him go back for it and told him to meet them at the party. Captain Crimson was extremely grumpy about being left behind. Thomas felt sorry for him, but they couldn't risk him bumping into Jeff.

Jeff arrived back at the café just as Gina and her friend were leaving. Jeff was horrified as he saw Gina give the man a big kiss.

"It was good to see you," Gina told the man.

Jeff backed away and tripped over a sleeping dog. He went flying backwards and landed with a splat in a large wooden barrel planted with flowers. Gina rushed over to help him up.

"You poor thing, you might have hurt yourself," she said kindly. "Why don't you let my brother drive you home?"

Jeff's mouth fell open. The strange man wasn't Gina's boyfriend after all! Jeff insisted that he was fine. With a cheery wave, he skipped into the café to collect Amy's cake.

Amy's party was in a sports hall. The games were being organised by Gary the Gladiator. He was a great big show-off. He'd brought some heavy weights to lift, to prove how strong he was. He asked if anyone wanted to try to lift one. He thought it was very funny when Whizz said she'd have a go.

"Are you sure?" asked Gary, winking at Amy. "I wouldn't want you to hurt yourself.

Whizz rolled up her sleeves. "I'll risk it, if you will," she told him.

Gary's jaw dropped as Whizz lifted the weight high above her head.

"Oh well," she said, "I'd better get on with the tea."

Whizz passed the weight to Gary. He tried to keep it steady, but his arms wobbled, his legs trembled and he staggered about. Then he fell over and banged his head. It made him see stars.

Just then, Jeff arrived with Amy's cake. He helped put an ice pack on Gary's sore head. The children were getting bored. Whizz told Jeff to organise some party games, so he asked if they would like to play Squeak Piggy Squeak. The children booed and threw beanbags at him. It was utter chaos. Suddenly, the hall doors banged open and in strode Captain Crimson. He had found a map that showed him how to get to the hall.

"Health and Happiness, people!" said the Captain. The children leapt up and down, cheering.

Jeff was very puzzled to see a real live Captain Crimson.

Amy raced over. "Listen everyone," she shouted, "meet 'Crimson' – our replacement Gladiator!"

Thomas was pleased that Dad believed the Captain was a party entertainer.

Captain Crimson leapt onto a space hopper.

"You'll never take me alive!" he roared.

Everyone grabbed a beanbag and chased after the Captain, who was bouncing down the hall. Amy gave the order: "Ready . . . aim . . . FIRE!" There was a shower of beanbags. The Captain jumped off the space hopper and onto a trampoline, which sent him flying through the air. He landed on a trolley, which slid along the floor and crashed into the tea table. The table tipped up, catapulting the Captain across the hall. He landed in a heap, upside down against a wall.

Amy's friends thought Captain Crimson was wonderful. Jeff rushed over to shake his hand.

"You saved our skins today!" he told him gratefully.

"No need for thanks, Sir," replied the Captain, wondering what day it was. "It's all in a day's work."

Chapter 5
It'll all come out in the wash

One morning, half way through the summer holidays, Jeff had a letter from Gina. She was inviting him to give a talk about his work at the library. Jeff was very pleased that Gina had thought of him. As the day of his talk grew nearer, he began to get very nervous. On the day, Jeff was in such a panic that he nearly left for the library wearing his pyjamas. Thomas had to take him upstairs and help him decide what to wear.

Meanwhile, Whizz was in the kitchen, struggling with a huge amount of washing. She'd promised to wash the tablecloths from the café, but she hadn't realised there would be so many. Thomas had finally managed to get Dad ready. He waved him goodbye and wandered into the kitchen. He couldn't believe the amount of laundry that was scattered about.

"It would be quicker to do them at the launderette," he pointed out.

"Thanks, Thomas," said Whizz.

Thomas looked shocked. "I didn't mean me, Whizz," he protested. "I'm supposed to be on holiday."

Jeff came rushing back in. He'd just remembered that today was Deadline Day and he hadn't finished his

Captain Crimson story. He told Thomas that he had made up a story, but he hadn't written it down properly. Thomas promised that he and Amy would do it after they'd been to the launderette for Whizz. Thomas couldn't believe that it was the summer holidays. He'd never worked so hard in his entire life!

There was an old lady at the launderette who looked after the machines. She sat in a room at the back. Thomas and Amy struggled to get all the tablecloths out of the plastic sacks. Captain Crimson didn't help. He was far too interested in the washing machines. He'd never seen anything like it before.

"Do people really come to this place to wash clothes?" he asked.

Thomas and Amy couldn't see what was so strange about that.

"All fabrics are self-cleaning where I come from," he told them.

Soon, Thomas and Amy were busy shoving tablecloths into machines. They didn't notice that Captain Crimson had stripped down to his underpants and was putting his clothes in a machine. The old lady came out of her office to see if Thomas and Amy needed any help. She took one look at the Captain and fainted.

Thomas and Amy helped the old lady back into her office. When they came out again, Captain Crimson was very pleased with himself.

"Look," he said proudly, "I've got all the machines going." The machines were making strange, gurgling noises.

"How much powder did you put in, Captain?" Amy asked him. Captain Crimson pointed to a huge stack of empty boxes.

"Captain!!" yelled Thomas and Amy together.

The noise from the machines was getting louder and louder. Bubbles poured out of the doors, slid down the side of the machines and covered the floor. Then the machines started clanking and clunking and rocking from side to side.

"How are we going to stop them?" wailed Thomas.

The Captain raced over to the nearest machine and tried to open the door. Thomas and Amy shouted at him to stop, but he couldn't hear over the noise of the machines. He forced one door open, then carried on and opened all the others. The two friends watched, helplessly, as the launderette filled with a volcano of bubbles. There were huge waves of soapy water and a messy tangle of tablecloths.

It took forever to mop up the bubbles. Then they had to wash the tablecloths again, to get all the soap out. It was late by the time Thomas, Amy and the Captain got home. They had to get straight down to work on the Captain Crimson story.

At the library, Gina was introducing Jeff to the Young Reader's Club. The children cheered when they realised that Jeff wrote the Captain Crimson stories. Gina sat at the front to listen. It made Jeff extremely shy. At first, he couldn't think of anything to say, so he showed the children how he drew their favourite hero. They all wanted to have a go. That made Jeff feel more confident, so he told them the story he'd made up for that week's Captain Crimson adventure.

Captain Crimson and his crew were on holiday at the seaside.

The volcanoes are about to erupt!

Widget thought he could smell smoke. When he looked up, he saw the volcanoes had flames leaping from their peaks.

Captain Crimson had to think fast. The Martian's village was about to be buried in boiling lava

Go and lead your people to safety, while we divert the lava flow.

As the lava blistered its deadly way towards the Martian's village, Captain Crimson was struck by an idea.

Quick! To the landing pods!

The crew flew straight towards the volcanoes. The metal on their landing pods began to melt.

The powerful surge of the thrusters blasted a ditch in the sand. In the nick of time, the deadly lava was diverted.

Captain, you're a hero! That could have been a disaster. All thoses Martians would have died.

I should have known you'd save us! How can I ever thank you?!

It's all in a day's work!

When Jeff had finished, the children crowded round him, asking for his autograph. Gina could see how much everyone had enjoyed his talk. She was delighted. So Jeff was delighted too. He started planning to ask Gina out. The Captain wasn't so cheerful, though. The story about being on holiday with his crew had made him terribly homesick. There was no doubt about it, he was starting to miss *The Galileo*.

Chapter 6
Take the bull by the horns

By the middle of August, things suddenly began to improve. Jeff was actually getting on with his work. He'd got his confidence back, once he realised that Gina liked him. He'd finished his Captain Crimson story ahead of time and was going to the library to ask Gina out on a date.

Even Captain Crimson had managed to keep out of trouble. He'd been spending his time trying to contact *The Galileo*. He was so fed up of not being able to talk to his crew that he'd built a home-made transmitter. But it wouldn't work. Whizz suggested that the transmitter might work better in the countryside. So Thomas and Amy helped Whizz to make some sandwiches and they took Captain Crimson for a picnic.

When Captain Crimson tried to contact *The Galileo* in the countryside, there was no reply. The Captain was very unhappy.

"I should imagine it takes a while for the message to travel through space," Whizz told him.

"I should imagine it's just not working," Captain Crimson replied, sadly.

Whizz tried to distract him by suggesting they have

their picnic. The Captain was always interested in food. Unfortunately, when he sat down to eat, he landed in a cowpat. He made everyone get up again to look for a better place to have a picnic.

They tramped about for ages. At long last, Captain Crimson led the others through a gate into a field.

"I want to eat here," he insisted. "There are no cows, no ants, no bees, no nettles – no nothing!"

Everyone decided that it was the perfect spot for a picnic. They walked into the field and the Captain shut the gate behind them. Nobody saw the large sign, which read 'Beware of the Bull'.

Jeff was in the library, trying to ask Gina out. He was so nervous that he wasn't making a very good job of it. In fact, he was doing so badly that Gina didn't know what he was talking about.

"Miss, Miss – he's trying to ask you out," explained a boy who had come in to borrow a book.

"Is he?" asked Gina, delighted that the mystery had been solved. "Well, if he is trying to ask me out, I'd certainly love to go."

Jeff was two galaxies beyond thrilled.

Captain Crimson had cheered up. It probably had something to do with the huge amount of food he'd eaten. There was a faint rumble in the distance.

"Oh dear," said Whizz. "Is that thunder? I hope it's not going to rain."

Amy and Thomas looked at the sky. There wasn't a cloud to be seen. The rumbling grew louder and louder, and then the ground started to shake. Suddenly, a huge bull appeared and came pounding towards them.

"Quick! Run!" shouted Whizz. Everyone jumped to their feet.

Whizz, Thomas and Amy tore across the field. As the bull charged, Captain Crimson stepped in front, waving his cape. When the bull saw the red cape, he stopped chasing the others and screeched to a halt. Then, he started pawing the ground with his head down. Whizz, Thomas and Amy watched from the far side of the gate. They were very worried about the Captain. But as the bull charged, Captain Crimson swept the cape aside and the bull ran past him.

The bull turned, ready to charge again. With a terrible bellow, he thundered towards the Captain. Captain Crimson flicked his cape to one side. With a surprised moo, the bull sailed on, missing Captain Crimson and landing with a tremendous splash in a muddy pond.

"I don't know how to thank you, Captain," said Whizz gratefully.

"No need for thanks, Whizz," replied the Captain rather smugly. "It's all in a day's work!"

They'd all had enough excitement for one day, so Whizz drove them back for a quiet afternoon at home. But when they got there, Jeff was out and the Editor had used up all the paper in the fax machine, complaining about the latest story. He said it was 'lovey-dovey rubbish' and that Jeff would lose his job if he hadn't written a new story by the end of the afternoon. Thomas decided they couldn't risk waiting for Jeff to get back. They'd have to write the story themselves.

The *Galileo* was on routine space patrol, when First Officer Optic noticed a large object travelling rapidly in their direction.

There's a meteorite racing towards us!

Take evasive action, Widget!

Optic calculated that the force of the collision would destroy everything!

There's only one hour left to save our world.

Millions of innocent people are going to die!

TIME TO IMPACT 60:00

The Captain came up with a plan that relied on split-second timing. He would pilot a space pod and jolt the meteorite off it's life-threatening course.

We must slow the meteorite down!

Captain Crimson bravely piloted his tiny spacecraft into the path of the mighty meteorite.

00:08

Nobody dared to move as Captain Crimson's deadly countdown began.

Stand by to transport in five, four, three . . .

00:07

The force of the explosion sent the meteorite tumbling through the atmosphere. It plunged straight to the bottom of the ocean.

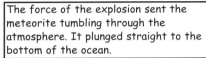

Meanwhile, Jeff was sitting in the park, daydreaming. All he could think about was that Gina had said she'd go out with him. Of course, he felt pretty bad when he finally went home and Thomas told him they'd had to redo his story. But Jeff did see the funny side when he realised how mushy it had been. Luckily, the Editor liked the new version and accepted Jeff's apology. Whizz and Thomas were really pleased that Gina had agreed to go out with Jeff. They couldn't bear to think what he'd have done if she had turned him down.

Chapter 7
Operation Recovery

There were only two weeks left of the summer holidays. Thomas was desperate to find a way of sending Captain Crimson home again. But before he'd had a chance to work out how to do this, Jeff caught a terrible cold. He woke up with it on the day of his date with Gina, which was a Thursday – Deadline Day. It was the only day that week that she was free to go out with him.

Whizz was in the kitchen when Jeff came in, looking terrible.

"Are you well enough for your lunch with Gina?" Whizz asked him.

Jeff replied that there were three hours to go until lunch.

"I'm going to get better by then, if it kills me," he told her.

He showed her what he'd just bought at the chemist's. It was a bottle of Sneeze Blaster Cold Cure. Whizz warned him that it might make him sleepy. She was worried that Jeff might not be able to finish his Captain Crimson story – or go out with Gina. The instructions said that you were only supposed to take the medicine at night.

Jeff told his mother to stop fussing. He was determined to get better straight away. Besides, he had loads of time to finish his work. He'd already done all the drawings and worked out the story. Jeff took some medicine. Then he took some more.

"Don't overdo it," Whizz ordered.

"As if I would," said Jeff, taking a really long swig from the bottle. "See, I feel better already," he mumbled, before passing out on the table.

Thomas knew that he and Amy would have to finish the story for Dad. They looked at what he'd done so far and decided that they shouldn't let the Captain see it. It was all about Captain Crimson suffering from a terrible illness. But the Captain forced Thomas to let him see the story. When he had read it, he gasped, clutched his chest and went quite pale.

"I told you I was ill," he wailed.

"Only in the story," Thomas reminded him. "In real life, you've just got a bit of a cold."

The Captain didn't believe Thomas. He decided that he was very ill indeed. Amy sent him to find Whizz.

Whizz took Captain Crimson's temperature. It was slightly higher than normal, so she made him an appointment to see the doctor. Now Captain Crimson was really worried. Whizz tried to calm him down. She told him that he only had a slight cold. It was nothing to worry about – unlike the Captain in the story that Thomas and Amy were writing.

The Captain and his Science Officers had been visiting Saharadon Seven. It was a barren, desert wasteland, where only a few heat-loving plants could survive.

What a beautiful flower!

Widget? Stand by to beam us aboard.

As the Captain stooped to sniff the exotic bloom, a cloud of foul-smelling dust unexpectedly shot into his eyes.

Be careful, Captain!

PUFF!

It's only a bit of pollen. I'm fine.

But Captain Crimson was far from fine . . .

Are you unwell, Captain?

THROB! THROB!

I do feel a bit peaky.

The Captain's behaviour was quite out of character. Optic ordered the guards to carry him to the hospital section.

...ack, Captain – ...e a sick man.

The flower was blooming. It was sucking all the liquid from the Captain's body. Unless they could stop it, he would die.

The Captain looks like he's at death's door!

Yes, I'm afraid he's fading fast.

51

Meanwhile, other members of the crew had been attacked by the mystery flowers. The fearless space crusaders had become a crabby bunch of bad-tempered children.

It's mine!

Na na nee na nah!

I saw it first!

It's spreading like wildfire!

We must find a cure, or we'll all die!

The only way to kill the desert flowers was to freeze them. Optic turned *The Galileo's* heating system off.

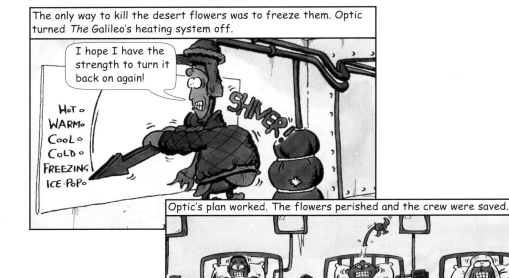

I hope I have the strength to turn it back on again!

HOT ○
WARM ○
COOL ○
COLD ○
FREEZING ●
ICE-POP ●

SHIVER

Optic's plan worked. The flowers perished and the crew were saved.

First Officer Optic was the only man left on board with the sickness. Dr Laser prepared to chill his body to a sub-zero state and cure him.

I don't know how to thank you, Optic!

Nnnno nnneed fffor tttthanks, Sir . . .

52

Jeff slept for most of the day, knocked out by the Sneeze Blaster Cold Cure. Whizz had to ring Gina and cancel lunch. Thomas knew that Dad would be utterly gutted, but there was nothing else they could do. Dad was still snoring his head off when Thomas and Amy took Captain Crimson to the doctor's. Amy sat in the waiting room, while Thomas went in with the Captain.

Dr Levy took Captain Crimson's pulse. Then he listened to the Captain's heart. He wondered whether he should get a second opinion.

"It's serious, isn't it, Doctor?" asked the Captain. "You can tell me – I can take it."

Dr Levy told Captain Crimson that he was a medical miracle.

"What are you talking about?" stammered Thomas.

The doctor replied that Captain Crimson had no pulse and he couldn't find even the hint of a heartbeat.

"He can't find a heartbeat!" gasped Captain Crimson, even though he didn't know what a heartbeat was.

Dr Levy said Captain Crimson had to go to hospital. "This man should be dead!" he said, ringing for an ambulance.

The Captain fainted, but once the shock had worn off, he was very pleased with all the attention. He waved cheerfully to Amy as he was carried out of the surgery on a stretcher. Thomas sent Amy home to fetch Whizz, while he went in the ambulance with Captain Crimson.

At the hospital, Thomas tried hard to get the Captain to leave. He was having such a good time that he didn't want to go.

"I have no heartbeat!" the Captain said proudly.

"Why should you?" asked Thomas. "You've come straight out of a comic!"

Amy arrived to say that Whizz was standing by with the getaway car. Captain Crimson said he couldn't possibly leave. He was standing by for an operation. Thomas and Amy were horrified. The Captain didn't understand why they were making such a fuss.

"I've been on hundreds of operations," he boasted. "They probably just want me to deal with some hostile aliens."

Thomas told him what a hospital operation meant. Now the Captain was frantic to go home.

Thomas and Amy raced down the corridors, pushing Captain Crimson in his bed. They were chased all the way by Dr Levy and a crowd of doctors and nurses. They only just managed to get the Captain out in time. With a squeal of tyres, Whizz drove Captain Crimson home to safety.

They arrived home to find that Gina had popped round with flowers for Jeff, so naturally he was feeling miles better. Which is more than could be said for Captain Crimson, who'd been terrified by his near miss at the hospital. School went back in a few days time. Thomas, Amy and Whizz had to send Captain Crimson back to *The Galileo* before then – but how?

Chapter 8
Black to the future

There was less than a week left of the holidays and Jeff was finally back to normal. His writing problems had completely disappeared after his date with Gina. The Captain, on the other hand, was utterly miserable. All he wanted to do was get back to *The Galileo*.

Whizz took the Captain to the local Science Museum to see if it would give him any ideas. Captain Crimson saw a space rocket and started to take it apart.

"You're not allowed to do that, Captain," Thomas told him nervously, as two guards walked towards them. The guards told Captain Crimson that it was forbidden to touch the exhibits.

"Nonsense!" huffed the Captain. "I'm a fully qualified Space Pilot."

The guards thought he was being rude. Whizz dragged Captain Crimson out, helped by Thomas and Amy. He grumbled all the way home, saying that he hadn't finished looking around.

Jeff had invited Gina round for tea. Thomas and Amy sneaked the Captain up to Thomas's bedroom.

"I may as well face the fact that I'm stranded here," Captain Crimson told them, sadly.

Amy begged him not to give up.

"We'll think of something, I know we will," she told him.

Thomas and Amy went downstairs for tea. The Captain wanted to go with them, but Thomas reminded him that Dad and Gina were down there. The Captain was fed up with having to stay hidden all the time.

Whizz made a fantastic tea and everyone enjoyed themselves. Thomas and Amy took a big plate of cakes up to the Captain, but the bedroom was empty. Amy found a letter that the Captain had written for them.

It said that he'd gone back to the museum. He wanted to see if he could get the rocket to take him back to *The Galileo*.

"We'll have to tell Dad," said Thomas.

But when Thomas tried to tell Dad what had been going on, it all came out in a muddle. Amy couldn't stand it.

"Whizz, the Captain's gone!" she shouted.

Thomas explained that Captain Crimson had gone to steal a rocket from the museum. Jeff was very puzzled. Thomas told him that Captain Crimson had been there.

"He's always here," said Jeff.

"No, in real life," said Thomas. "He's been staying in the house."

Thomas and Amy wanted to go after the Captain. Jeff said he couldn't work out how to help unless he knew more about how Captain Crimson had got there in the first place. Thomas told him all about the day the ink spilt and how Captain Crimson had arrived through a black hole.

"Why can't Captain Crimson go back the same way?" Gina asked.

Everyone looked at her as though she were crazy.

"If Jeff drew another black hole, perhaps the Captain could use it to get back to his ship," she explained.

Jeff reminded Gina that the first time it had happened, Captain Crimson was near a black hole himself. Then Whizz remembered that there was a black hole exhibition at the museum. If they could get the Captain into it, while Jeff wrote an ending with a black hole, then they might be able to send him back again!

Jeff sent Whizz off to the museum with Thomas and Amy, while he and Gina stayed in the house to work on the story. It was half past four. They had an hour to find the Captain and get him into position before the museum shut for the night.

At the museum, the Captain was trying to get the rocket started. He flicked switches and twiddled knobs, but he couldn't make it work. Then he noticed two guards walking towards him. He hid until they had passed. The others found Captain Crimson trying to move the rocket. Lights flashed and alarm bells rang.

"RUN!!!" the Captain yelled.

Suddenly, the guards appeared up ahead. Whizz grabbed Amy and ran to the left. The Captain grabbed Thomas and ran to the right. They hid as a guard went past. The guard was talking into his radio. They heard him say that the museum closed in five minutes. Thomas had to get the Captain to the black hole exhibit, or they would never get him back to *The Galileo*.

Gina was pacing up and down in Jeff's studio while Jeff worked on the last picture. She warned him that he only had a few minutes left. Jeff promised that he'd get the picture finished in time.

Thomas and the Captain were running along, when Thomas noticed a sign for the black hole exhibition. A clock on the wall showed that it was nearly half past five! Then a guard jumped out at them.

"Come back here!" the guard yelled, as they ran through the entrance to the black hole exhibition.

"Shut the door, Thomas," ordered the Captain. "We'll barricade ourselves in!"

Captain Crimson dragged a chest across the door.

"There's only twenty seconds to go, Captain," shouted Thomas. "Get into position. Now!"

Captain Crimson raced to stand in the museum's

black hole. Suddenly, his transmitter crackled into life and for the first time in weeks, Captain Crimson spoke to the crew of *The Galileo*. The crew were locked onto his coordinates and were standing by to beam him up. The guards were banging on the door. Thomas struggled to keep it shut.

"Hurry!" he shouted. "I won't be able to keep them out for long!"

"I don't know how to thank you for everything you've done," Captain Crimson told him.

"There's no need for thanks, Captain," Thomas smiled. "It's all in a day's work!"

Tiny flashes of light began to sparkle and dance around the Captain's body. He was waving goodbye to Thomas as the door burst open and Whizz, Amy and the guards tumbled in. They all watched in amazement, as Captain Crimson slowly faded away to rejoin his crew.

Captain Crimson and Widget were returning from an external inspection of *The Galileo*, when the Captain unexpectedly vanished.

The members of the crew were frantically worried about the Captain. They tried to contact him, but there was no response.

One minute he there, the next was gone!

Optic glanced at the main screen and realised at once what must have happened. The Captain had been sucked into a black hole!

What shall we do now?

The crew had no choice but to follow the Captain into the black hole. It was an incredibly dangerous operation.

DANGER

NO TRESPASSING

KEEP OUT

The Galileo would have only two minutes to find the Captain before the starship was sucked into the centre and destroyed.

We're taking a huge risk.

But it's for the Captain!

As Widget entered the data for their dangerous journey, the ship's computer suddenly burst into life. Warning messages instantly blared through the ship

Stop that noise immediately!

WOOP! WOOP!

CLANG! CLANG!

Changing to manual override.